T0130127

THE BRIDE FROM THE DEPTHS

THE BLUE LAKE

CORNELIA CALAIDJOGLU

THE BRIDE FROM THE DEPTHS
THE BLUE LAKE

iUniverse books may be ordered through booksellers or by contacting:

iUniverse
1663 Liberty Drive
Bloomington, IN 47403
www.iuniverse.com
1-800-Authors (1-800-288-4677)

ISBN: 978-1-5320-9313-5 (sc)
ISBN: 978-1-5320-9314-2 (e)

Library of Congress Control Number: 2020900638

Print information available on the last page.

iUniverse rev. date: 01/23/2020

UNDERWATER
BRIDE

A young redheaded woman with a complexion as white as an open soul interlaced the thread of her fate in a dreadful untouched realm. In the floating cells of her red blood, nonpareil feelings boiled like a flood of unspoken words. A simple wedding dress and a circlet of natural wild flowers resting delicately on her head made up her outfit.

In tears, her spirit told me about her destiny under a vaulting, dead sky. She left matter and life, believing that the water would be soothing for her longing, and appointed me the sole master of her living spirit.

The circlet stayed scented on the surface of the lake, spreading deep melancholy like a long-lashed maid. A night like a disturbing story became the cure for the burning fire, and her latest decision was her last. The petals of the flowers and the pistil kept their fragrance, sending hazy signals to the waves of unbridled love. Days and evenings were late, hidden in the sunset, and the darkness set its seal like a grip over the soul's rays. Lateness chose a throne sticking its roots deep into the underwater tomb.

On a cold evening, about 150 years ago, Dumitru—urged by his engineer friend, Tudosie—bought the southern area of Câmpina, which was rich in oil. Settled in a hilly area, the small village had a few hardworking people. Scanty houses and narrow streets wound through the buildings. The villagers were used to experimenting with small businesses, especially in agriculture and beekeeping. Therefore, huge prospects were envisioned in the continued evolution of the community. Dumitru—urged by his friend who was an expert in the oil field—moved there.

While waiting for the completion of his house, a mansion, he lived almost half a year with Tudosie, who had become like a brother to him. He wanted a baroque-style home with a strong emphasis on carved walnut furniture. After many long days and nights of waiting, the project was finished. Once the house was ready for dwelling, the rich ornaments and luxurious stretches reflected grandeur and majesty.

"Thank you very much for your hospitality and accommodation, dear friend," said the landowner, shaking his hand in gratitude.

"My house is also your house," Tudosie replied.

"Whenever you need me, day or night, my door will always be open to you."

The keeper asked, "Can you call Geta to help me get my things together?"

"Of course I can," Tudosie said.

Geta—an elderly, serious, and diligent lady—was in charge of the chores. She had never had a family of her own. The only close relative she knew of was her nephew, and he had left the country. He rarely visited her during the holidays, and Geta felt he always went back home too soon.

Geta was a short, stocky woman with very curly light-brown hair. She spoke little and only when spoken to. Her black-speckled eyes called attention to her hard work and sleepless nights that were consumed with overwhelming thoughts. She had never met her parents. They abandoned her and her twin sister when they were less than three months old.

Elena, the twin sister, did not enjoy her life too much. She died while giving birth after her uterus ruptured during labor. Elena's husband remarried immediately after her funeral. His new wife did not want the baby, so Geta raised her nephew on her own. Geta never smiled after her childhood. She would look at people with a frown and was always annoyed. If you did not know the sad story of her life, you would have thought she had something against you. Despite her appearance, she was a warm, merciful, noble soul who was always ready to help. For Dumitru, she was like a mother while he lived in his friend's home.

Dumitru hugged his friend and left for his new home.

Assisted by two villagers, he marched up to his palace. His night was disturbing, and he was in a hurry to put his dirty plans into effect as soon as possible. He was tortured by the desire to get rich, and the darkness turned into malicious pleasures. No one suspected anything. He changed in silence. By day, he used to wear the mask of a gentle, noble, and generous man. He wanted to attract the peasantry to his side, and he would soon succeed. In the six months he spent in the village, he carefully and gingerly inspected the people's behavior while making inquiries about their customs and way of living. Most of them were poor and indebted. *Favorable ground*, he thought greedily.

At first, he offered them food and money. A diabolical plan was born and grew rapidly in his ravenous mind. He soon became one of the richest inhabitants of Câmpina. An army of servants contented themselves with the remnants of the goodies and rags, which for him constituted garbage, and they satisfied his snaky desires. He had a miraculous power to manipulate their minds.

Dumitru constantly regarded his title and wealth as magical controls that he deserved over the goods and over the whole world. He painted the walls of his life and existence in gold. The rest of the people and their souls were just dust and mud. Their needs were invisible walls for the greedy landlord.

White and yellow water lilies were floating on the blue lake where Ruxandra and Răzvan used to meet when they were very young. When she was sixteen, on a night with a full moon, Răzvan approached her, grabbed her by her thin waist, pulled her toward him, and kissed her for the first time.

Shaking, she said, "What are you doing?"

"Nothing bad! I love you, Ruxandra. You are my universe and the reason for my time. You are my music and my sunrise. You are my evening and my midnight tears. You are the red-haired fairy in my dreams, who pops up and disappears unexpectedly. I give you my life with all that it is. I would kiss the ground behind your steps, and I would build our sandcastle. I would defend it with my being, and I would not be afraid of the thunder in the storm or allow the night to scare me. Losing you is my deepest fear. I would poison it with kisses and plunge it into the depths of water."

With her large eyes, Ruxandra stared at him. She felt like she was looking at a ghost. Răzvan had never spoken to her like that before. She had a bad feeling; one she could not fully understand at that time.

He held her against his chest, more loving than ever.

Her frail, chaste, teenage body became anxious, and her thoughts were controlled by strange sparkles. *It's my evening*, she thought, resisting negative emotions. "Let's go. I want to assimilate this unique moment in the heart of my destiny. I will sing at my wedding."

They had known each other since early childhood. They ran barefoot in dusty clothes, laughed, played, and sang on the streets of the village, which had never been paved. They were like happy and carefree angels. They were desk mates in elementary classes, and they dearly remembered the pranks they played with the other kids. Time seemed to fly before their eyes; they grew and fell in love with each other. They planned to be husband and wife and to have two children: a girl and a boy.

Răzvan wanted the girl to look like him and the boy to look like her. "I want him to have the color of your eyes and their gaze." He was excited about this thought almost all the time.

"What will their names be?"

"Cătălin and Cătălina," he replied every time.

A fierce wind and a fiery red cloud came over the lonely hill on the outskirts of the village where they met. Fearing a violent thunderstorm, they ran hand in hand to their homes. He saw her to her gate, waited for her to get inside, and then ran like a lawless, giddy brigand past the ridge on the edge of the road to his house.

The hills came under the attack of the storm. Cold rain ruthlessly rattled the sheet roofs and rushed over the forest and helpless grassland. The animals hid in their homes and stuck their heads out from time to time with frightened gazes. The grass began to smell fresh, and the flowers opened their petals. The blue lake in the distance roared and rumbled with raging water.

Ruxandra put her pillow over her head. Persistent worries and thoughts bothered her. The dark ghosts were directed toward Răzvan.

In the middle of the night, he felt an inhuman emotion and became very nervous. As if pushed from behind, he rushed to Ruxandra's house. Dressed in a mint-green raincoat over a thin cotton T-shirt, he stood motionless in front of her gate for more than an hour. There was a frightening darkness all around, and all the lights in her house were off. When he finally settled down, he went back to his house, looking down like a careless hermit. He went straight to his bed and fell asleep with a thumping heart.

"Wake up, son. It's after seven o'clock," said a soft voice in the morning. "It's time to get ready to go to the field to help your father. We don't know the extent of the damage from last night's storm. I made your breakfast."

Still sleepy, he got out of bed, hurriedly splashed cold water on his face, and sat at the table. His father had finished eating and was preparing the cart and horses. Răzvan had a quiet breakfast and thought about his girlfriend.

"Maria, put more snacks in the saddlebag. We don't know how long it will take to finish work because there is a lot to do."

Razvi's[1] father came from Transylvania, and he kept the dialect of the region in his speech. He had met his wife at a baptismal party in his village in the north of the country. The young man immediately proposed to her because she was a sedulous woman, very kind and faithful. They had enjoyed a beautiful and peaceful marriage for twenty years. They worked hard and built a small household that provided them with a decent daily living.

Ruxandra's house was old. It was the next to last house at the end of the village. To the right, the way led to Doftana Valley, and to the left, you could see the thick beech forest.

Ruxi[2] had created her own piece of heaven in the household garden. In a corner were the most beautiful and exquisite flowers with lovely smells and colors. She had a cool room with the window facing the garden. Next to her room, two more bedrooms faced each other. They had lattice windows and lush greenery. Old-fashioned furniture occupied most of the rooms.

Her father, Puiu, was a rough and tough man. He

---

[1] Short form of the name *Răzvan.*

[2] Short form of the name *Ruxandra.*

used to hit and punish her mother, Marcela, and Ruxi whenever he had the opportunity. Puiu had alcohol problems and used to spend time at the village pub. He would come home drunk and was always ready to fight.

Her mother tried to defend her because Ruxandra was a kind child. But sometimes Ruxi's mother could not cope with her husband's violent outbursts. She would take her daughter and lock them in Ruxi's room to escape the aggressive man's anger.

Puiu did not like to work either. Marcela was the one who ran the house and sewed pillowcases and woolen blankets to sell at the fair. She bought necessities with the money she earned, and she never borrowed money.

The new morning looked like a yawning, sleepy child with a simple and cheerful nature.

There was quite a stir and hustle on the crooked, twisted lanes of the settlement. Some people hurried to the field with shovels on their shoulders, ready to work the land, and others headed to the fair with noisy animals. Children with backpacks headed to the village school.

Dumitru watched as his mischievous purpose was achieved. He told the villagers and his assistants to ask which peasants would like to help him process the black gold on his estate.

At the time, most of the people worked hard in the fields. They made a living by cutting and hauling wood in carts that were drawn by horses or oxen. They cut the trees into firewood or carved it into decorative objects, which they took to the fair and sold to the rich.

The landlord wanted those free peasants as slaves. They were very poor and lived in houses made of wood or earth. They used ovens and stoves to heat their rooms and cook their food. They baked breads and cakes with kneaded dough. Those who were a little wealthier raised pigs, cattle, geese, or turkeys. They killed them, smoked the meat, and stored it in an attic or cellar until winter when country life was even harder.

The devious landlord's ruse raged outside his cold black eyes like a sharp weapon; anyone could see his hypocrisy. Just down the hill, he was relaxing comfortably in his mansion, which was composed of three levels: a basement, the ground floor, and the second floor. While he was relaxing, he was thinking the best way to attract them as soon as possible. They worked on his estate from morning until evening. They ate whatever they could whenever they could. Some of them had neither home nor family; they woke up at dawn and worked without breaks for fear of being driven out of the mansion.

Many nights, Marcela, Ruxandra's mother, cried because her husband was good for nothing. When she heard that a local tycoon was looking for people to work she said to Puiu,

"Stop being lazy. Get dressed and run to the mansion on the hill for Tudor's sons, your uncle, and the neighbors across the street. Niculae's George, the guy who was working with the hives, went there as well. Ruxandra has grown up. If we had some extra money, we could send her to a better school in the city."

Puiu did not care about his daughter. His only concern was doing nothing except wasting time telling bad stories and drinking with other guys like him.

In Ruxandra's dark room, musical demons lined up and danced in a ring. The unknown wrapped around her, lured her into an anonymous, forced adventure, and captured her in its frightening, nightmarish claws. The passion was left behind, and her body trembled at the sound of water and grumbling voices.

Severe anxiety accompanied her, and she felt fear in every part of her body. She had a panic attack and was frightened by the unexplained emotions. She suspected something bad was going to happen to her. She found comfort in Răzvan's feelings. She believed they were from the Almighty and would defend her and protect her from any evil. She remembered their dream wedding. It had a lot of guests, many bouquets of red flowers, bridesmaids dressed in pink, decorated chariots, and fiddlers.

Răzvan felt anxious, and a deep deception invaded his gentle soul. Ruxandra was in his thoughts.

"Ruxi, are you okay?" he asked her during one of his panic attacks. Răzvan was a distinguished young man, and his nobility was not about money. He sincerely loved her and planned to propose to her when she turned eighteen the next year. He wanted to marry her because she was the most beautiful and brightest girl in the village. Despite her father's habits, she was educated. He knew he could never love another girl so deeply. *She or no one else*, he used to think.

On a chilly afternoon, a long line of men stood at the landlord's gate. They were waiting to close the deal with him. He was a white-haired aristocrat with a few bald spots and a long, bushy mustache with the tips twisted upward. His straight, imposing stature promised financial security.

One of the men waiting was Ruxandra's father. He was more groggy than sober. Gloomy, he decided—at his wife's insistence—to pull his own weight. The landlord was standing at the threshold of the door. Everyone could see the pride of the rich nobleman. He was accompanied by Tudosie.

Tudosie told the assembled crowd that Dumitru had great projects coming up. He wanted to set up the first refinery in the country—and in the world—with materials from Germany. He assured everyone that they would be rich in gold and money. The work would begin the next morning. According to Tudosie, the oil engineer, they would start digging ditches. Cables would be installed in the ditches, and pipes would be mounted.

The landowner had two hundred hectares of oil fields at the end of the village. He wanted to build a modern refinery on a surface of twelve hectares with the help of Tudosie and the sixty workers who accepted his offer of employment. The land was prepared very carefully, and the materials were on the road from Germany to Câmpina. The workers, pipers, and locksmiths were also prepared.

A new day was born. The sky opened above the Prahovan village, and the sun rose like a simple bouquet of yellow roses. It seemed to be an icon of simplicity.

While Dumitru was busy with his business, Ruxandra and Răzvan met at the blue lake. They were surrounded by dreamy reeds that were adorned with white lilies. The turquoise sky reflected on the water, and it looked like a fairy tale.

"Ruxi, let's throw a penny into the lake and make a wish." Răzvan was beaming with happiness.

"Come on," Ruxandra replied excitedly.

"You first" he said politely.

"Okay!" Ruxandra threw a coin into the calm waters and made a silent wish. "Now it's your turn!"

Răzvan made a wish, tossed the coin into the lake, and turned to Ruxandra. Her beautiful eyes were as green as an emerald. He whispered, "I love you, darling. You're wonderful and beautiful!"

The water began to bubble, and a strange howling in the forest sent chills down his spine. He did not move and was stunned with horror; only he could hear it. The boy turned green and looked as if he had seen a ghost. His breathing became jerky and fast. He was scared. He quickly breathed in deeply, but he felt like a fire was boiling in his body. Thousands of troubling thoughts invaded his mind, but his blood calmed when the unusual emotions died down. He tried to smile to avoid upsetting Ruxandra.

They ran to Răzvan's house. His mother, Maria, had the table ready for them. They had a chicken and rice dish, vegetable soup with cream, homemade cake with sour cherries, and grape juice.

While they were having lunch, a new feeling of concern sprang up in Răzvan's soul. A mixture of enigmatic feelings and prescience held him captive in their fierce claws for a few seconds. Hindered by mystical thoughts, he became pale and shocked. The unknown forces punched him deep in his young soul and sent alarming signals. His gaze blurred, and he looked sick.

Ruxandra noticed, panicked, and spilled her grape juice. "I apologize." She stood up from the table and looked for a napkin to absorb the spilled juice. "Răzvan, what's going on with you? Are you feeling all right? You are a little pale. Does something hurt?" She did not know why Răzvan looked like he was going to faint.

Răzvan did not want her to know about the inner demons that had been tormenting him for more than two weeks. He gathered his remaining strength and said, "I feel good, my love. It's most likely indigestion from the food. Please do not worry. I feel better now."

Ruxandra looked nervous and politely asked Răzvan to see her home. "It's late, and my parents are waiting for me." She turned to Maria and said, "Have a nice day!"

"Kisses, beautiful girl. Take care," she replied with a smile. "We are waiting to see you again."

Night was falling over the village, and the doors of the houses were locked. The darkness was like an angry young man; the light refused to be his bride, and he covered the heavenly vault with his rotten palm. The stars were hidden, and the sky was black and moonless. The hill plunged into a blind night, and the water kept glittering with insane cravings. There was no one in the streets: no creature, human, or stray dog. The village was wrapped up in a ghostly, grave silence. A strange night overshadowed the land. The earth seemed numb and lifeless, and only a black abyss survived in the universe.

It was getting light. It was a lazy morning, and no one wanted to wake up. Ruxandra awoke from her deep sleep and fled to Răzvan's home. She knocked on the door and entered his room. He was still in bed.

"I had a strange dream," she said.

"Go on. Tell me. What was the dream like?"

"I dreamed that war had started. You joined the army and left for the battlefield. It was a terrible world war. You were on one of the trains full of soldiers heading for the front lines. In my dream, it was winter—and you were frozen."

Răzvan smiled and said, "It was just a dream. I am by your side, and I will never leave you." He hugged her.

Ruxandra believed him and began to feel safe.

"Let's go to the kitchen and tell my mom to make us some milk coffee. Do you want some?" he asked.

"I do."

"Good morning, Mrs. Maria."

"Good morning, my girl. Sit at the table. I'm preparing you some breakfast."

They ate in silence and looked at each other with warm smiles.

Maria made them omelets with salted cheese, toast, mint tea sweetened with honey, and milk coffee.

"Thank you for the meal," they said.

"To your health, my dear ones."

As Maria cleared the table, the young couple stood up and got ready to leave.

"Let's go see my dad," Ruxandra said. "He's working for the proud landlord who built that great mansion at the bottom of the hill. He's building a refinery. Dad has been working with him since last week."

"Let's go," he said.

They crossed a cobbled alley with great care because the road was along a dangerous valley. It was a shortcut to the outskirts of the village where there were many people. There was a lot of noise since the construction of the industrial unit was in full swing. Since there were so many people, Ruxandra barely managed to see her father. When she saw him, she waved.

The construction had started on the tank parts, the fitting, and the furnace mounting.

"Hello, Dad!"

"Ruxandra, what are you doing here?"

"I came to see you."

"I can't talk to you too long. I have to get back to work. Here, complying with the work schedule is crucial."

"Okay, Dad. I won't hold you back. Good job!"

"Goodbye, Mr. Puiu."

Ruxandra was glad that she got to see her father working. While they were on their way home, the famous landlord rode by in a beautiful carriage. It was covered in gold and precious stones, was drawn by two superb horses, and was driven by a famous coachman from the village. Dumitru was dressed in a dark black tuxedo and a high-top hat that gave him a stylish, elegant look.

When the carriage went past them, Ruxandra looked down, embarrassed.

Dumitru could not take his eyes off the gorgeous redhead. He fell in love with her. He began to wonder who she was and whose daughter she was because he had never seen her before.

"Draghici, the redheaded girl who just passed us, do you know whose daughter she is?"

"No, Master," the coachman replied. "I haven't seen her before." Thousands of uncontrolled thoughts and unanswered questions began to sprout in his mind. A suspicion that he did not want to be real was ravaging his whole being.

"Who is the young boy who was accompanying her? Is she engaged? Does she love someone else? No, no, it can't be true! I'm delirious! She is single, and she will be mine!"

The landlord was a nervous wreck for days—from dawn until evening. He constantly wondered, *Is it possible to see her again or to speak to her?* He felt like he was going crazy. A quiet, frightening laugh echoed and gathered all of the evil spirits hopelessly seeking a ray of light. He wiped cold drops of sweat from his forehead and angrily hurried to the kitchen. He took a glass from the cupboard, filled it with water, and breathlessly drank the cold liquid.

A torrential rain came ripping through the forests and meadows between the hills.

At night, Ruxandra heard a fascinating and captivating voice. It seduced her, and she allowed herself to be carried away. She left her house in the middle of the night like she was sleepwalking. Ruxi was barely clothed. As if she was hypnotized, she headed for a slippery, damp marsh.

In the forest, many birds were screaming. They sounded as frightening as angry dogs barking. She looked straight ahead without turning to the left or the right or the back. She was carried away by the spell and hoped it would accompany her to Răzvan. She arrived near a mysterious blue lake, and vipers had their beds on the muddy shores. A flute song sounded sweet.

The snakes left their hiding places and began dancing around her. They curled up on her thin body, and purple lightning struck over the cursed water. A snake with dark scales raised its head, hissed wildly, and spit black venom from its wide-open mouth.

Ruxandra was startled and felt like the spell was breaking. She felt weak-kneed and extremely dizzy, but then she woke up from the nightmare. With wide eyes, she screamed in horror. The terrible place was as dark as coal. She lost her balance and fell to the ground. With her right hand, she held a branch of a short tree. Almost breathless, she crawled with the last of her strength to the only bench in the alley. On her hands and knees, she grabbed one of the bench legs and tried to get up.

A new morning broke above the leaves, and the fruit was covered with fresh dew. An amateur fisherman saw Ruxandra and went to help her.

She had fainted, and her head was hanging to the side.

The fisherman picked her up.

As though by magic, she opened her eyes and looked at the man who was carrying her.

The brave fisherman put her on the bench and let her drink water from a green bottle.

"What is happening to me? Where am I? Why am I here?"

"Girl, you fell on the grass near the bench over there."

He pointed to the spot where he had found her. "What are you doing here at this time of the day? You fainted, but I picked you up."

"I do not know why I am here. I should be home in my bed," she mumbled, barely able to speak.

"What is your name, girl?"

She did not easily understand the question, and it took a great effort to remember who she was. "My name is Ruxandra, and I want to go home."

"Do you feel like you can get home?"

"Yes, if I stay calm. Thank you for your help. I am grateful to you." Wishing to get home as soon as possible, Ruxandra—lost in her thoughts and lost in space—took the shortest route. She carefully entered the yard without making the slightest sound. There was absolute silence. The chickens were sleeping, and even the wind was still. Her parents were still in their room, and she tiptoed into her room. After a while, she heard her father's steps in the kitchen.

Puiu took a bucket and went out to get water from the well. He washed his face in a small blue basin and went to work without even having a snack. Punctuality for the avaricious landlord was the law.

Dumitru did nothing except ask everyone in the village who that wonderful girl was. Anyone who found out her identity was to tell him immediately. After many days of searching, he found out about the young lady's brief conversation with Puiu near the main installation. Without thinking and not caring about anyone or anything, he went to Puiu and said, "Is the girl who came here a few days ago your daughter?"

"Yes," Puiu replied in a trembling voice. He feared that he would be admonished.

With a stunning gleam in his eyes, a glow of radiance appeared on Dumitru's face. Once he learned that the girl's father was a servant of his, he began to behave nicely to him. Dumitru radically changed his attitude toward Puiu.

One day, Dumitru asked Puiu to meet him after work. He said it would be a great pleasure to visit him at his home for a chat. He convinced Puiu that he was very involved in his employees' lives—and Puiu should not hesitate to ask for help or support.

Puiu accepted right away. He had no idea about the deviant thoughts in the covetous man's mind. He also cared very little about his daughter. Though she was his own flesh and blood—and she was a good daughter who loved him dearly—she was the last person he cared about.

Under a full moon and a clear, fairy-tale sky, Dumitru's chariot arrived at Ruxandra's home. He was dressed in a simple yet elegant outfit.

The coachman got out of the chariot and opened

the door like a servant. The whole scenario was set up perfectly to justify his presence and the unexpected visit.

Surprised, but happy at the same time, Puiu said, "I didn't expect to see you tonight, Mr. Dumitru."

Ruxandra's mother was fascinated by the landlord's presence in their humble home. She rushed to light the fire and cooked a quick dinner for Dumitru, which he ate with a good appetite.

Ruxandra was reading a book in her room.

Ruxandra's mother said, "Ruxi, please come, dear, and help me bring these cake trays to the table. We have a guest. Come and say hello to him."

Ruxandra was shy, but she carried the plate of homemade sweets. She politely greeted him half-heartedly.

When Dumitru saw Ruxandra, he felt like screaming for joy. She was so close to him. *Finally! Finally!*

In his house, Răzvan felt restless, and terrible memories were dragging him down. The same stormy feelings and hollow emotions were shaking his young soul. A bad omen crept into his heart.

Marcela, Ruxandra's mother, had made plum brandy, and Dumitru let a few slugs of the brandy flow down his throat. He told Puiu that he did not have to go to work the next day since the refinery was almost ready. All that was left to do was check the equipment. To look generous and to gain his confidence, he offered Puiu a monthly salary. It was like an unemployment benefit.

Puiu, a lazy man, accepted the offer on the spot. They had another glass of brandy to seal their deal. "Ruxandra, more brandy, please." He was excited to earn money to buy more liquor and just stay home.

After dinner and several glasses of wine and brandy, Dumitru was satisfied with his success. He wished them a good evening and went home. He fell asleep quickly on his expensive sheets.

Bright stars adorned the night sky. Ruxi sat on the porch and admired the spectacular view and the colors and the intensity of the light. She sat in the same place as her ancestors did centuries ago as they gazed at reddish stars that changed in color and intensity from time to time. Ruxandra was tired and went to her room. It was small but beautifully decorated with craftsmanship from Muntenia. She opened her window and slept until dawn.

For the next few days, the landlord's loyal coachman brought food, clothing, and many other gifts to Ruxandra's family.

Ruxandra considered the gifts help from the nobleman, and she was always happy to receive them. She was deeply grateful and wished good health and a long life to his generous soul.

On a sunny afternoon, Ruxandra and Răzvan met in

the glade by a rocky road. They sat on a blanket on the grass under a tree. The perfume of the wildflowers was dazzling.

Răzvan picked red, yellow, violet, pink, and blue flowers and made a wreath that he placed on her temple. Birds with brightly colored feathers and emerald-green eyes fluttered under the vault of light. Fields of sunflowers and ripe corn were unfolding in front of them, and their eyes were invaded by the decorative yellow. The crickets were competing to see who the lead singer would be. Red ladybirds with black dots and yellow ladybirds with white dots rested on the blades of grass. It was a heavenly sight, and their love had the distinction of the queen of the universe. Smiles like twin princesses were on their graceful, elegant faces. They unpacked their bag of fruit and shared it with each other.

"Here you go! Have a pear!"

Ruxandra took a bite from the tasty fruit and said, "It's so sweet!"

"It's not sweeter than you!"

Ruxandra blushed and looked down.

"My sweet! You look so good with the circlet on your head! You look like a fairy."

Ruxandra's waist-length red hair was shining in the sun.

On Tuesday at dusk, Dumitru sent Tudosie to Ruxandra's home to get Puiu and personally escort him to his place.

"Marcela, make some coffee for Mr. Tudosie."

Puiu hastily got dressed and rushed to the landlord's home with Tudosie. Behind the gate, there was a large semicircle yard. It was surrounded by a board fence and shaded by poplar, acacia, and walnut trees. On the right side of the yard, there were the farm and barns, and on the left side of the yard, there were vineyards and gardens with colorful flowers. The pink roses were the most beautiful and fragrant.

Dumitru had hidden many coins and old objects of great value in the cellar. No one knew about it. The cellar door was locked, and no one else had a key.

An army of servants lived in the adjoining house. It also housed the kitchen where all of the food was prepared. The cook was a tall woman with an olive complexion, big green eyes, a long, full face, and red lips. She was smiling with satisfaction. She had no other goals in life. She always wore a head scarf. She had well-worked hands with long fingers and short, well-groomed fingernails.

There were flocks of geese, turkeys, and chickens

everywhere. The servants worked from dawn to dusk. Dumitru's home was quiet, populated, and clean. The rooms were spacious and furnished with elegance and refinement. The house had the most coveted style in the world. There were artistic, dramatic paintings of mystical characters with bronze, silver, and gold finishes on the walls.

The dining room was for honored guests and renowned fiddlers. The handcrafted chairs and tables were made from the highest-quality walnut. The pillows on the chairs were covered with purple velvet. The sofas were decorated with drawings of flowers, angels, and shepherdesses.

Dumitru invited Puiu to sit down at the table, which was full of goodies.

Puiu remained silent as he stared at the wealth and gold. The old wines on the table were the first ones he wanted to taste. He had never seen so much expensive alcohol in his life.

A short and thin servant filled two glasses with brandy and brought them to the table on a tray.

"Cheers again," Dumitru said in a loud voice. "Good luck! And because we are here in my house, I will tell you something." He looked Puiu straight in the eye. "What would you say if we were relatives?"

"How?" Puiu asked.

"Come with me, and I will show you something."

They went down to the cellar, and Puiu looked around and shuddered.

"Look at this treasure! All of the gold here, all of the coins, and everything else will all be yours if you accept my proposal."

Puiu, slack-jawed, said, "What would I have to do to gain so much wealth?"

"You do not have to do very much," Dumitru said. "I just want you to give me your daughter in exchange for all of this wealth. I will also give you the two houses on the hill and the entire orchard by the field."

"I accept," Puiu said immediately. "Ruxandra will be your wife! I think she will be very happy when she finds out." Puiu had sold his daughter without any moral consideration, remorse, or pity. He did not even think about the fact that Ruxandra had just turned twenty—while Dumitru was in his sixties!

Dumitru said, "The refinery is up and running, and the oil extraction has started. We processed it, and we have already started to export it. I am not immortal." He was trying to sound convincing. "If we become relatives and Ruxandra is my wife, then all that I have is hers. This house would be yours too. I have no other heirs."

Out of the blue, a pitch-black mist covered Ruxandra's beautiful eyes. She felt numb. The darkness sharpened its claws and summoned evil demons to attack. A cold sweat violently flooded her body. She could hardly breathe, and she smelled fear in the room. The end had the appearance of a lake, and she could feel it approaching. She felt like she was floating above the blue water. She was wearing a princess's wedding dress that was embroidered with fine lace and tightly tailored for her body.

Răzvan was in bed. A deep silence surrounded him. He felt like everyone else was trapped in a grave sleep. A painful cold pierced his heart. The old gas lamp spread a dim, yellow light. Răzvan burst into a dreadful, desperate, uncontrollable cry. Sitting on the edge of his bed, he screamed in pain and hid his face in his hands. Tears cascaded from his eyes, and fear roamed around his gaze. He felt like he was waiting for the end. After a couple of hours, the sighs finally ceased in his trembling body.

In her room, Ruxandra sat in an armchair by the window. The beautiful view was like a painting. The banks on the horizon were covered in a white haze, and clouds galloped in slow motion over the celestial waters. The natural flow of her thoughts suddenly stopped. Emotions gripped her, and she knew she could not remain conscious for long. In her mind, she saw an isolated place surrounded by flowering trees. There was a special silence.

Ruxandra felt a terrible, ominous hatred sparkling in her tired eyes.

Puiu came back home just after eight o'clock and yelled, "Ruxandra, come here right now!"

Ruxandra's universe turned to fields of fire and flooded forests.

Her father approached her and smiled mockingly. "Get ready for your wedding." He was babbling and laughing. "No one will know how rich I am now. You will be the wife of the most famous man in the village." He looked like a hungry wolf who wanted to tear his prey apart. "You will marry the richest man in the village. You will obey. I gave you life—and I could kill you!"

Rumbles of thunder screamed in the night sky and invaded her thoughts. In the background, she heard two violins. She was delirious. She put her hands over her ears and ran down the street like a ghost in the middle of a dark storm. The white-yellow flowers of lemon verbena weaved hope and carpeted the damp ground. In the distance, the splashing blue water rang like a bell. She felt like she was walking in quicksand as she headed toward Răzvan's house.

Dumitru's eyes glittered in the night as he gazed at Ruxandra's picture. The stars were shining and waiting for another morning.

In his room, Răzvan was moaning and crying. His tears turned into bloody red beads.

A suffocating darkness fell over the village. On the table, the flame of the old candlestick started flickering and sizzling—and then it suddenly went out.

The angels of the night were shivering in the countryside.

Ruxandra knocked on Răzvan's door!

Răzvan wiped his tears with his sleeve. "Who could be here at this hour?" He rushed to open the door. "Ruxandra! What happened? Has your father kicked you out again?" Seeing her, his thoughts no longer hurt him. He was home alone since his parents were visiting a relative in the capital.

Ruxandra was pale and exhausted from everybody and everything.

"Come in, Ruxi." He gently took her hand. Barely suppressing his panic, he said, "What happened? Sit down and tell me."

Ruxandra burst into tears. She was crying from fear, fatigue, and confusion. "Dad … wants me to marry that old man who has the refinery." Her voice was trembling, and she could barely tell him what had happened.

"No!" he screamed. "No! Let's run away, Ruxandra. Wait for me to grab some clothes, and we will leave!"

Attacked by another wave of pain, she buried her face

in Răzvan's shoulder and whispered, "I can't. Take me home, please."

The days and nights felt like they would never end. Răzvan's life felt like a bad dream. He felt like he was fading away in the branches of the walnut trees that had been planted in the garden of his house on the day of his birth. Puiu had forbidden Ruxandra from seeing him anymore. Răzvan decided to stop acting like a child when he heard the news. More than ever before, he wanted to act like an adult. He wanted to face the injustice with an adult's strength of character and fight for their love.

Dumitru felt free to visit Ruxandra more and more often. Meeting her hateful, contemptuous gaze, the flame in his eyes pierced her heart with sorrow. Whenever she thought about Răzvan, her soul flooded with deep love.

Under the gray autumn sky, the two soul mates' shattered dreams began to dig heavy bleeding wounds. Nature was getting ready for its winter sleep in the Prahova Valley. Copper-colored leaves fell from the trees and covered the ground with a rust-colored carpet. It was the same color as the young couple's tears. Without their leaves, the trees seemed hopeless—just like the couple's long-desired hugs.

Two years had passed, but Ruxandra still refused to marry the man she was sold to. She secretly met Răzvan under a full moon.

The wet and sad autumn wind began to blow from the misty hills, bringing echoes of muffled rumbles on its wings.

Then there were rumors of war on top of the villagers' everyday struggles. When the war did break out, the Romanian army joined the battlefield. Thousands of carts loaded with food for the soldiers left for the front lines and returned with human remains. Some of them were so disfigured they could not be identified. The soldiers' bodies were buried in the village's military cemetery. Their graves were marked with white crosses. The words "Unknown Homeland Hero" were written in large letters.

"Mother, it's time for me to join the war," Răzvan said. With a resolute smile, he added, "For my country."

His mother started crying. "And endanger your life? Can you not see there is mourning in the village? Can you not see the children in the street waiting for their fathers to come home from the war?"

Răzvan ignored his mother's questions. He kisses

Ruxandra's picture, put it in an inside pocket of his jacket, and left for Timisoara. He went to the recruitment center, and a tall colonel with a chestnut mustache congratulated him. Răzvan put on his helmet and uniform, which had been provided by the French. Răzvan proudly looked in the mirror and saluted.

After Răzvan attended artillery school for two months, he was sent to the front lines. They made him an officer due to his courage and devotion. He was injured three times. The last time he was seriously injured, he had to stay in a hospital for two months. He wrote a letter to his mother and said, "We only understand the value of life when we are facing death—and the danger and bloodshed only strengthen our soul."

She replied, "God willing, it finishes one day. May the Blessed Virgin help us. We keep looking out of the window, watching and waiting for you to return home. I hope you will come back home safe, my dear. My heart is heavy, and I feel my blood boil as I worry about you. There is so much fussing here in the village as the injured soldiers cry in a tent because there is no room in the hospital for them. We start each day fearing that something bad may happen to you. Ruxandra has been sad since you left. She did not marry that rich man, and she is waiting for you to return. She has seriously lost weight longing and crying for you. Write to her to comfort her, my dear. She is getting sick with so much grief and anxiety."

Nine months after the outbreak of the war, the Romanian front lines were filled with blood, graves, dead soldiers, and piles of tear-stained letters from mothers and wives. The wounded soldiers' groans and wails mingled with the roaring of the earth, which was eager to take their bleeding bodies. Razvan fought courageously on the front lines, and his heart was noble and devoted in those hard times.

In another letter, his mother said, "Since Romania entered the war, our life is even bitterer. We have no food or medicine. We agreed to take care of a major. He is a very good man. He was injured in his left hip. The hospitals here are full of wounded soldiers. They sent him from one hospital to another, but there were no free beds for him. We volunteered to take care of him here at home. He sleeps in your room. A nurse comes to check on him from time to time to clean his wound and change his dressing. He has just been operated on and is recovering well."

From a bloody trench filled with piles of corpses, Răzvan wrote, "We will win one day! Do not worry, Mom. Kiss Ruxandra for me and tell her that I love her dearly. I will write to her if I have time. I will be home soon."

It was dark, and the clouds were dancing lazily. On his way to the train station, Răzvan met two tall, thin men in black. They were coming from the front lines and pushing carts with wounded soldiers. Răzvan greeted them and hurried through the rails, which were glowing like two endlessly long swords. He looked to his left and could only see fog. He looked to his right, and the darkness brought the sky and earth together. Panting and barely able to walk, he continued on toward the train station.

Răzvan was waiting for the train that took soldiers to the front lines. The crowded train was puffing and whistling as it left the mountains behind. The locomotive looked like a monster from another world as it blew smoke, creaked, and slowly chugged along. The windows were opened when it stopped at the station. The soldiers in the corridors huddled together and waited to get off the train.

Ten very young soldiers unloaded war equipment from another wagon.

Răzvan said, "Officer Răzvan Adumitriei."

A soldier with a twisted black mustache said, "Long live! I am Lieutenant Tănase Mihai, and I am the leader of this group. I will lead you to the Romanian front lines. They are waiting for you. As I call your name, please let me know your medical condition. With so much bloodshed, we must try to prevent the spread of any diseases. Follow me. This way!"

Răzvan followed the short lieutenant across a muddy street with bloody puddles and out to the battlefield.

The way to the battlefield was not easy. Soulless bodies that had once been vivid, brave soldiers, covered the ground. Many of the wounded and grieving survivors were missing arms or legs. Some of them were transported in carts to nearby hospitals, but others were not so fortunate. Soldiers were donating blood on the battlefield for those who had a chance to live. They were crying and screaming because they wanted to go home. Some of them had young children or sick parents to take care of.

While Răzvan was caring for two of the wounded soldiers, he heard a loud bang. He rushed to the bombed area to rescue those who could be saved. As he was running, he was shot in the head. He collapsed to the ground. Blood was gushing from his temple and pooling on the ground. In a short time, he breathed his last breath. He was a hero of his country and worthy of his oath.

His mother wrote to him every day for three weeks, but she never received another answer. When she heard that Răzvan had lost his life on the front lines, she screamed in anguish and pulled her hair. "I want him at home—even though he is dead. Why doesn't anyone bring him to me?

My boy, my little boy." A cascade of tears flowed from her hollow eyes.

Ruxandra ran to her sweetheart's house. His mother was crying loudly and pulling her hair.

Răzvan's father had been on the front lines for more than a month.

Răzvan's mother said, "Ruxandra, dear, Răzvan is no longer with us. He was shot and killed."

Ruxandra screamed like crazy and fainted.

Vasile, the wounded major, carried her weak body to the bed. He sprinkled cold water on her face, and she began to blink. Her face was yellow, and her gaze was unfocused. "Pick yourself up, dear," he said. "You are young. It's a shame for you to fall apart like that! May God give you the strength to overcome this misfortune that has come upon you. God forgive him."

For four months, Ruxandra cried all day and all night. She cried on the shoulder of the woman who was supposed to have been her mother-in-law. Each day, they lit a candle at the village church and prayed to God. They hoped it was fake news—and Răzvan would return home safely—but it was not like that at all.

The cold days and nights passed. Marcela and Ruxandra felt their souls melting like snowballs in the heat of the sun. Weeks and months passed, and the bloody war finally ended. There were more women than men in the village. There were also more children and older people than young men or boys. They did not return home from the Romanian front lines. They had died for their homeland. It did not matter if they died from a bullet, the weather, hunger, blood, loss, or disease. No matter what the cause was, the result was the same.

In the rush of life and facing hard times, Ruxandra wanted to stay away from her father's violence, fury, and insistent pressure. She decided to accept the greedy old man's proposal and said, "Dad, I will marry Dumitru."

"Finally, you made the good decision," he said in a cruel voice. He had sunken eyes, red cheeks, and a swollen belly. In his harsh gaze, his desire for insane achievement glittered. Ruxandra had barely finished speaking before he hurriedly put on a coat and rushed over to Dumitru's mansion to give him the long-awaited news.

Above the hill, the sky seemed to meet the blue lake. The lake stretched out and seemed to accommodate a creature that spread its arms and screamed like a leafless tree losing its fruit in a splash of foamy smiles.

The silence sounded like an echo, and Ruxandra's soul cracked. She slammed the windows shut, and the wind admired her with the tenderness of a poem. A chill crept into her room, and angels spread their icy wings in the secrets of their voices.

Ruxandra quietly tried on her wedding dress. She was

beyond words. Her teary soul crumbled into thousands of pieces—like little feathery stars that she gathered in her palm and blew away.

Night fell over the wounds of the earth, and Ruxandra fell into a deep sleep. In her dreams, she saw Răzvan. He was as handsome as she remembered. They were walking hand in hand through an alley of fragrant flowers. Butterflies with multicolored wings got their nectar from the flowers.

Răzvan bent over, picked a flower, and gave it to her without letting go of her hand. In a tender, loving voice, he said, "My love, I'm here in heaven. I love you more than ever, my bride. Do not move forward. Do not … do it only if you do not love me anymore."

Ruxandra woke up at dawn—dazzled by the dream—and smiled lovingly.

At Dumitru's mansion, the wedding preparations were almost complete. The guests, wearing their best clothes, were getting ready to arrive at the church by the lake. They were supposed to arrive at lunchtime.

The fiddlers had memorized the songs and were eagerly waiting for the party to begin.

At ten o'clock in the morning, Ruxandra sent her mother to the field to pick some flowers for her. She was going to braid a circlet for herself.

At noon, Ruxandra put on her simple wedding dress,

which was tailored tightly to her thin body. She placed the circlet of natural wildflowers on top of her frail head.

A sparkling carriage was waiting for her in front of her house. The four beautiful racehorses had flowers on their ears.

Dumitru wore an elegant brown silk tailcoat and top hat.

The delicate bride, holding a bouquet of white flowers, got in with her mother. The carriage—also adorned with carefully chosen flowers—was proudly driven through the streets of the village.

On the road in front of the church, dancers were holding each other's waists tightly. The wall of bodies was winding, bending, and twisting to the fiddlers' music. The more they took delight in the dancing, the wilder and more alert the music became. The boys were jumping, leaping, and stamping their feet.

In a whirlwind, the dancers' wall took a plunge. The fiddlers animated the dance with rhythmic shouts and verses, and one of the dancers answered them. The row of dancers tightened and curled like a snake. As they were slowly uncurling, they showed off their red, cheerful faces. A crazy rhythm broke out like a fury of human passion.

Ruxandra was dancing in the center of the ring, and Dumitru was spinning her to the left and to the right.

The dance became slower, which irritated the fiddlers.

They began to play harder and louder, and the dance became stormier. It looked like they were digging into the ground with their feet. They were a row of curling and uncurling bodies.

The bells were ringing at the church, and the young people were scattered around and laughing savagely.

Suddenly, Ruxandra disappeared like a ghost. She floated over the dancers as they performed movements that were as old as the hills. The blue lake unbraided her hair and kissed her white forehead. It lifted her in its arms—more soothingly than ever before—and took her across the threshold of the depths. Her circlet stayed scented on the surface of the lake, spreading deep melancholy like a long-lashed maid. Burning flames were muffled in the water. The petals and pistils of the flowers kept their fragrance and sent hazy signals to the waves of unbridled love.

A deafening noise from the depths greeted the ears of the people. They were staring at the circlet floating in the glow of the light-blue water. Relaxing music and the sounds of nature, birds, and the forest came out from the underwater tomb.

The outraged crowd turned their eyes to Dumitru, but he was stiff with fear. He was shaking and looking around. His heart shook, and he felt the eyes of the people piercing through him. He felt cold and anxious. He pulled the collar of his coat over his bare neck, grabbed the edge of the top hat, and pulled it over his eyes. He did not want to see anything.

Puiu was totally drunk and couldn't comprehend anything that was happening around him.

When the crowd found out that Ruxandra's father had forced her to marry Dumitru, they started booing and cursing Dumitru and Puiu. The people were getting restless.

Dumitru saw a little girl on the dark ground. She was holding Ruxandra's bridal bouquet. He rushed home, locked himself in his room, and sat down in an armchair.

The wind was beginning to blow, and the rain was approaching in the air. Soon, through the rustling of fallen leaves, Ruxandra's spirit breathed and was relieved.

Dumitru seemed calm and peaceful, but he had gone insane. The man who had been so domineering now refused food, and his eyes were empty and fixed. He was scared of the light, and he heard voices at night. His hands shook, and he completely stopped talking. That was the end for him. His servants finally felt free. They talked with Tudosie, the only person who was close to Dumitru, and decided to put him in hospice.

Today, the inhabitants of Câmpina say that Ruxandra's veil can be seen floating on the lake on rainy evenings.

A Romanian archaeologist discovered Răzvan's

remains near the International Heroes' Cemetery in Valea Uzului. A black-and-white photo of Ruxandra was found in his backpack. The letters, yellowed by the passage of time, had been written a century ago. Răzvan Adumitriei had lost his life in World War I. His name was inscribed on a tablet along with the military unit to which he belonged. The Romanian army held a commemoration ceremony to pay tribute to him. They named him a hero of the homeland and left twelve wreaths on the place where he was found.

Printed in the United States
By Bookmasters